The Longest Hair
in the World

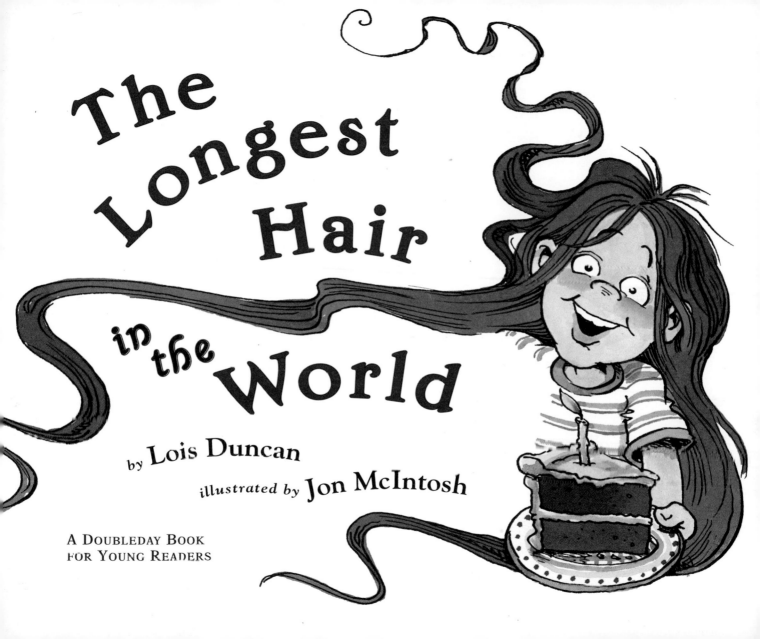

The Longest Hair in the World

by Lois Duncan

illustrated by Jon McIntosh

A DOUBLEDAY BOOK
FOR YOUNG READERS

A DOUBLEDAY BOOK FOR YOUNG READERS

Published by
RANDOM HOUSE, INC.
1540 Broadway, New York, New York 10036

Doubleday and the portrayal of an anchor with a dolphin are trademarks of Random House, Inc.

Library of Congress Cataloging-in-Publication Data
Duncan, Lois.
 The longest hair in the world / by Lois Duncan ; illustrated by Jon McIntosh.
  p.   cm.
 Summary: On her sixth birthday, Emily wishes for the longest hair in the world, and as it continues to grow and grow it creates terrible problems for her and everyone around her.
 ISBN 0-385-32113-9
 [1. Hair—Fiction. 2. Wishes—Fiction. 3. Birthdays—Fiction.] I. McIntosh, Jon, ill. II. Title.
PZ7.D9117Lp   1999
[E]—dc21   98-53072
                                             CIP
                                             AC

The text of this book is set in 15-point New Aster.
Manufactured in the United States of America
October 1999
10 9 8 7 6 5 4 3 2 1
PHO

For Zoe Palmer with love
　　　　　—L.D.

　　　　　　　　For Forgan and Hays
　　　　　　　　　　—J.M.

I t was Emily's birthday.

She stood gazing down at the sparkling candles on her cake.

"I wish I had very long hair," said Emily. "I wish I had the longest hair in the world."

Then she blew out the candles—every last one.

"What a silly wish!" said her mother. "Short hair is so easy! Why would you want very long hair?"

"Our class is having a play," Emily told her. "The girl with the longest hair will be the Princess."

"There are lots of long-haired girls in your class," said her father. "Your hair can't possibly grow longer than theirs that fast."

"You never can tell," said Emily.

When Emily woke up the next morning, her hair was down to her shoulders.

Two days later, it was down to her waist.

By the end of the week, Emily had the longest hair in the class.

"Emily will be the Princess," said the teacher. "The rest of you long-haired girls will be ladies-in-waiting. The short-haired girls will be pages, and the boys will be dragons."

The boys cheered!
The short-haired girls looked disappointed.
The long-haired girls were so mad they burst into tears.
"Emily's cheating!" they screamed. "She's wearing a wig!"

One yanked Emily's hair to see if it would come off.
That girl had to spend the rest of the day in Time Out.

Emily's hair kept growing. By the night of the play it was so long that the pages carried it onto the stage like a train.

The audience applauded.

"What incredible hair!" they shouted.

"It's going to be a bother to take care of," said Emily's mother.

Emily's hair was so long that she couldn't get it into the car. Her parents drove home alone, and Emily took the bus. Her hair took up so many seats that the driver charged extra.

The next day Emily's father traded their car for a convertible. Now Emily's hair could stream out behind it. Other drivers pulled their cars off the road. They didn't want all that hair to get stuck in their windshield wipers.

Emily had fun trying out hairdos.
Sometimes she wore braids.

Sometimes she wore curls.

When Christmas came she made her hair twinkle! "We don't need a tree," bragged her father. "We have Emily!"

But as Emily's hair kept growing, it began to cause problems. When she went to bed there was so much hair in the bedroom that her parents couldn't get in to kiss her good night.

"This hair must be trimmed!" exclaimed her mother. "A mother has to be able to kiss her own child!"

She got out her sewing scissors and cut Emily's hair. By morning it had grown back even longer.

Emily's father rearranged the furniture so that her hair could hang out the window. That worked well in the winter, but in the spring birds discovered the hair and built nests in it.

It was summer before the baby birds fluttered from their nests. By then Emily's hair was pretty awful.

"I told you long hair would be a bother to take care of," said her mother.

Emily had too much hair to fit into a washbasin or a bathtub. Her hair would not even fit into a neighbor's swimming pool.

"I have an idea!" said her father. He drove the convertible through a car wash. Suds flew in all directions. Huge brushes whirred and spun through the tangle.

Water poured into the car and gushed over the sides. Emily sputtered and spat. "I'm drowning!" she shouted.

"You made the wish," snapped her father, "so stop complaining!"

Emily spread her hair on the lawn to dry. A man from a gardening service came to rake out the snarls.

"That was a hard day's work!" he grumbled at quitting time.

Emily's hair continued to get longer.

In the autumn it collected red and yellow leaves. When the leaves turned crunchy and started to smell funny, Emily's father drove her back through the car wash.

Emily found out that having long hair could be lonely.

She wasn't invited to her friends' houses. Their mothers were afraid she would shed on the carpet.

At school she had to do her lessons in the cafeteria. Her hair wouldn't fit in the classroom.

Nobody wanted to play with Emily at recess. Her hair got looped in the swings. It got tangled in the jungle gym. And when Emily got on the seesaw, her end of the board stayed down, no matter how many people piled on the other end.

The class put on a new play, but Emily wasn't in it.
"This is a play about dinosaurs," said her teacher. "In dinosaur days there weren't any princesses."
The boys and the short-haired girls got to be dinosaurs. The long-haired girls stood behind them and sang songs about dinosaurs.

The fire department said Emily's hair was a fire hazard. She wasn't allowed onstage. Instead, she sat behind a curtain and made dinosaur noises.

Nobody knew who was making them. The applause was for the dinosaurs.

Then one day it was Emily's birthday again.

Her mother lit the candles and cried, "Enough is enough!" She set the birthday cake in front of Emily. "Like it or not, I insist that you wish your hair short again!"

Emily sighed. She knew her mother was right. Her hair could not keep getting longer and longer. After a while there wouldn't be room for it on the planet.

"I wish my hair was back like it used to be," she said. "Instead of long hair . . ."

The cast for the school play was soon to be decided. The play was about a porcupine named Spikey. Only one lucky child could be the star.

"Instead of long hair, I wish . . ." Emily closed her eyes. ". . . I wish I had quills. I wish I had the longest quills in the world!"

Her father and mother screamed, "Don't!" but before they could
stop her . . .

Emily blew out the candles—every last one.